Gladys

Martha

ALBERT

WHEN THE THE MICE

LIONEL

MARTHA'S CAT'S AWAY WILL PLAY

CONTRA COSTA COUNTY LIBRARY

Houghton Mifflin Company Boston 1995

When you go off to school,
you think I just sleep all day.
WELL, BOY,
HAVE I GOT NEWS
FOR YOU!

I have my own newspaper delivered to keep myself up-to-date with the goings-on in the cat world.

I keep myself fit to make
sure that the dog next
door can't catch me.

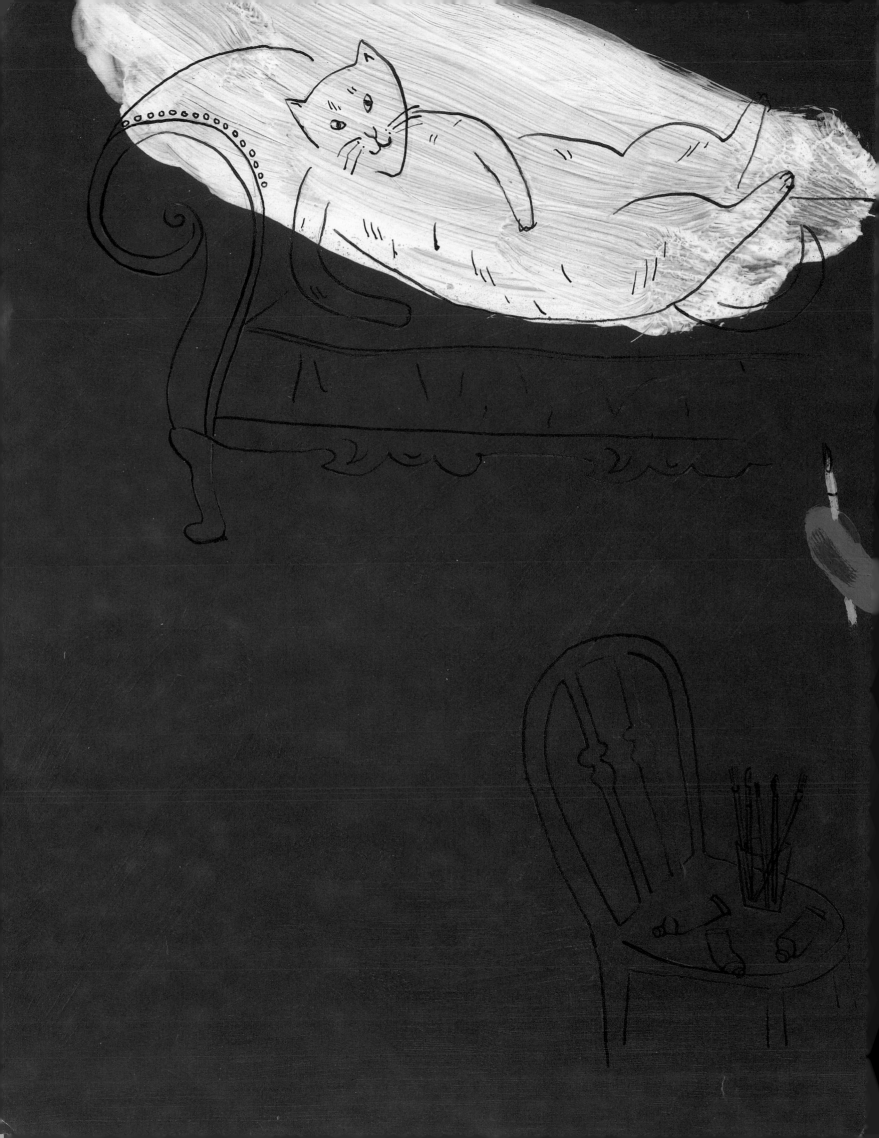

At ten o'clock I set up my easel and paints and *Gladys* from No. 34 poses for me.

I cook myself some lunch.
My favorite is a nice bit of salmon washed
down with a cool saucer of milk.

I like to watch the cartoons
while I have my lunch.

I phone my cousin **ALBERT** in Atlantic City for a chat.

Sometimes in the afternoon Flash Harry
knocks on the back door with his suitcase
full of goodies.

I have a little nap and, WOW,
do I have some good dreams.

I listen to the radio. I like the gardening programs that tell me all about the plants and flowers in our garden.

Then I go upstairs to get changed for my afternoon performance.

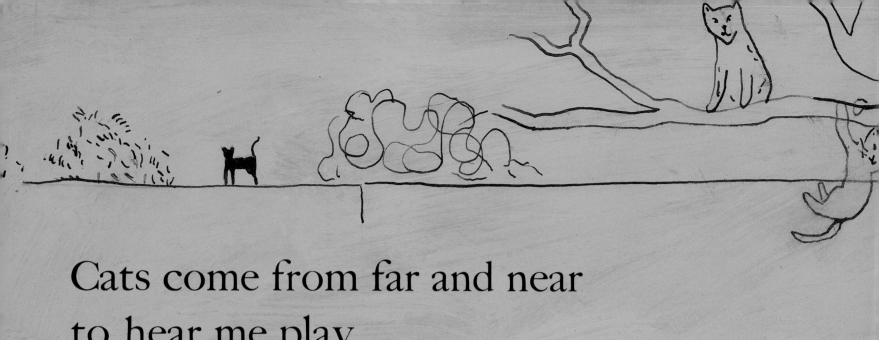

Cats come from far and near
to hear me play.

They are very
generous with their
applause and I usually
do a couple of encores.

I play with your toys. *Audrey* from across the road comes over quite often to play doctor.

If there's any time to spare, I take the car for a quick spin around your room.

When I hear the garden gate, I dash downstairs to the sofa and pretend to be in the Land of Nod. Then you rush into the room and kiss me hello, thinking I have been asleep all day.

Well, now you know!

*This book
is especially
for Jessie*

Copyright © 1995 by Bruce Ingman
First American edition 1995
Originally published in Great Britain in 1995
by Methuen Children's Books

Library of Congress Cataloging-in-Publication Data

Ingman, Bruce.
    When Martha's Away/Bruce Ingman. — 1st American ed.
        p. cm.
Summary: Martha thinks her cat sleeps all day, but nothing could be
further from the truth, as the cat himself reveals all his daily activities.
        ISBN 0-395-72360-4
        1. Cats — Fiction. I. Title.
PZ7.I486Wh 1995
[E] — dc20

                                        94-36582
                                          CIP
                                          AC

Flash Harry

Audrey

Flash Harry

Martha